D0791840

I AM A BIRD

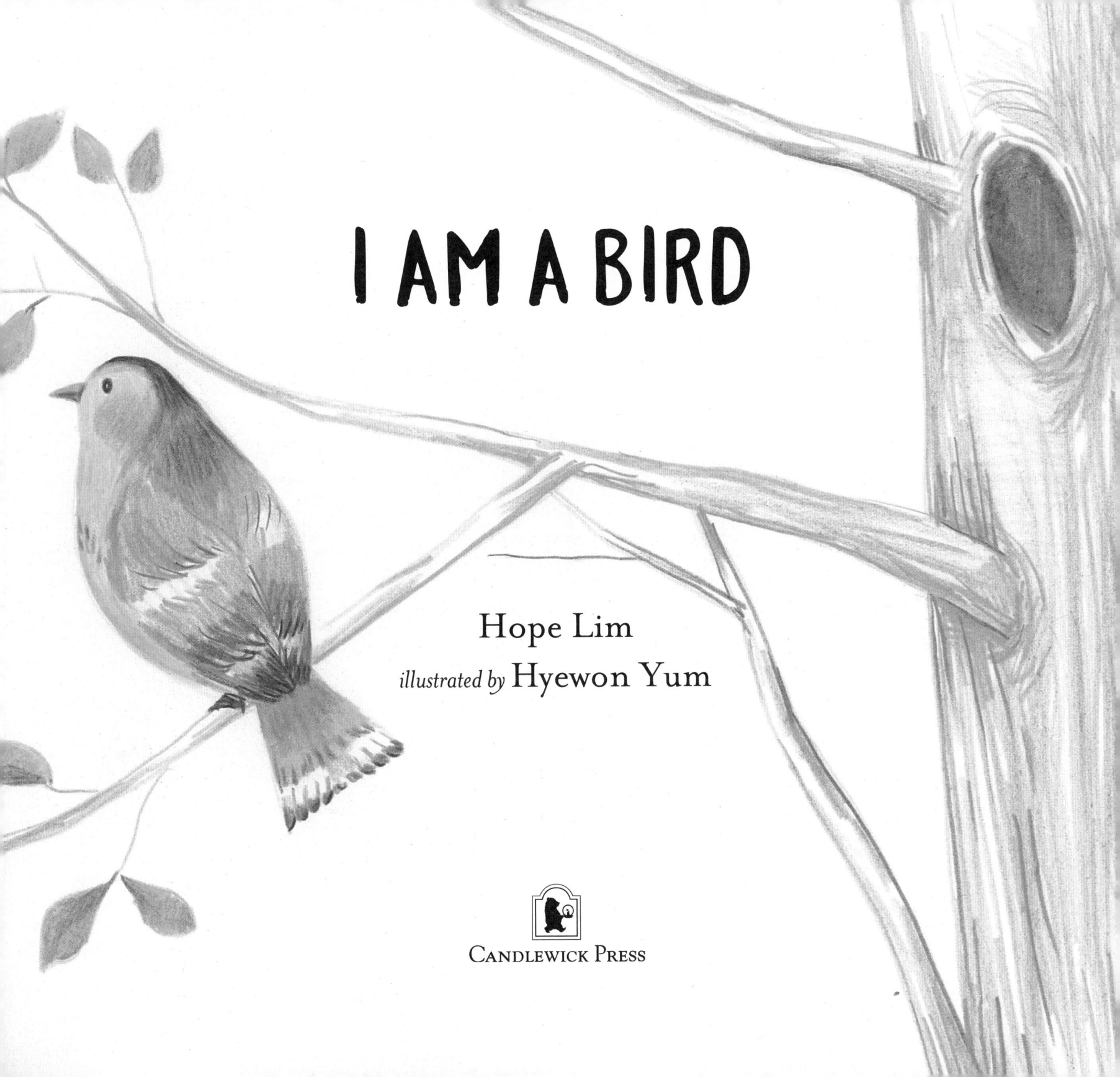

I AM A BIRD

Hope Lim

illustrated by Hyewon Yum

CANDLEWICK PRESS

주차
금지

I am a bird.

Every morning, I fly like a bird on Daddy's bike.

I sing like a bird on the way to school.

People wave and smile,

and the birds sing back.
CA-CAW!

One morning, I see a woman
with a blue coat and a big bag.
She is walking very fast.

세탁
개조심

She does not wave.
She does not smile.

The next morning,
I see her again
with the same blue coat,
the same big bag.

I do not smile.
I do not wave.

I turn and look
and wonder . . .

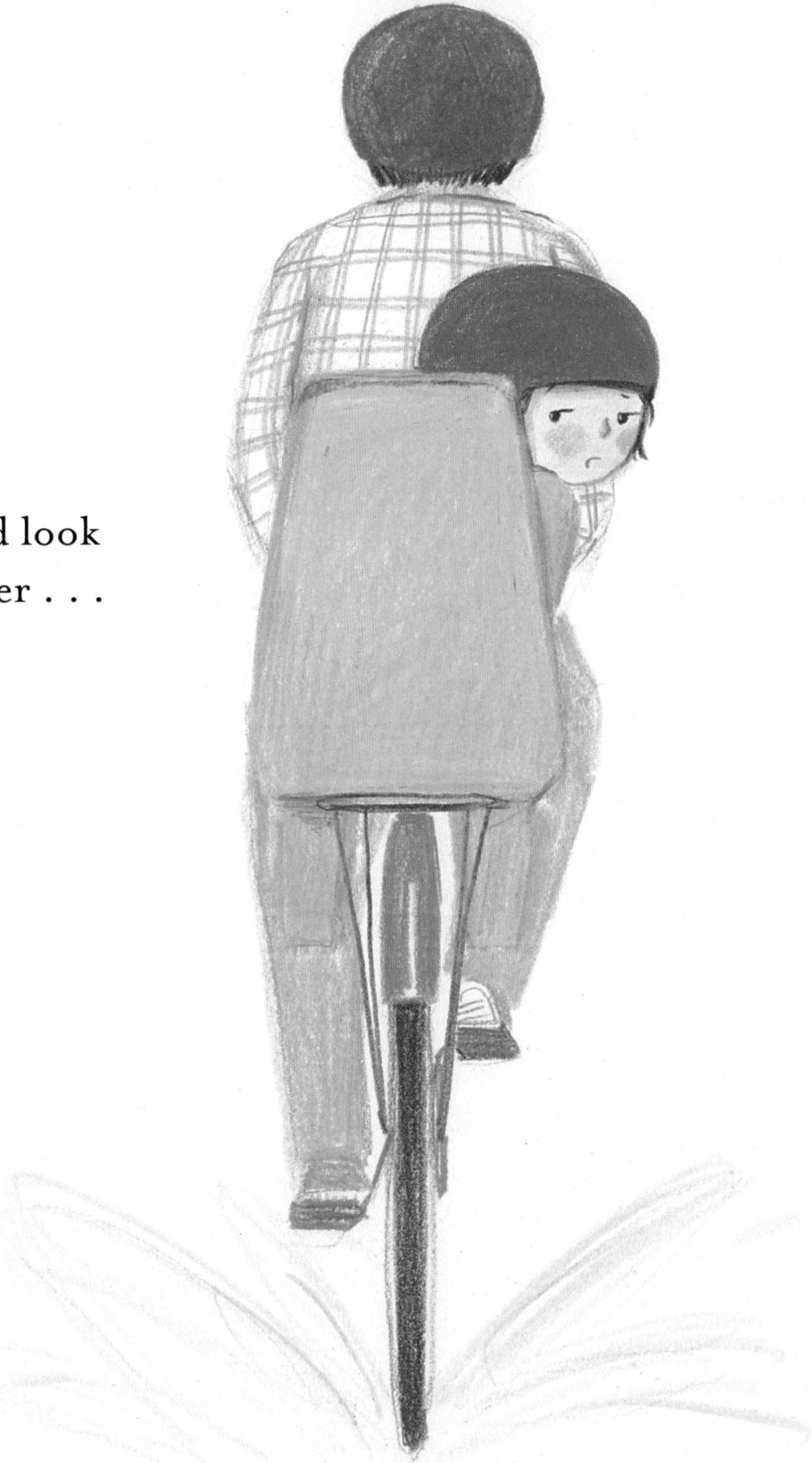

What's inside the bag? Where is she going?

Why doesn't she smile and wave?

Day after day, my birdsong stops
when I spot the blue dot in the distance.

"Daddy, I don't like her."

"She's just a lady taking a walk."

But what if she's not?

I hide behind Daddy's back when we pass her.

One morning, we are late for school,
and we don't pass the woman.

Then, near the end of the park, I see her.

When we get closer, I hear her . . .
CHEE-
CHEE-
CHEE . . .

She's whispering a song to the birds!

I turn and look until she sees me.
I smile and wave.

CHEE-CHEE-CHEE...

I am a bird again.

And now I know she is just like me.

We are birds.

For Sophia, my soaring bird
HL

For my mom
HY

Text copyright © 2021 by Hope Lim
Illustrations copyright © 2021 by Hyewon Yum

All rights reserved. No part of this book may be reproduced, transmitted, or stored in an information retrieval system in any form or by any means, graphic, electronic, or mechanical, including photocopying, taping, and recording, without prior written permission from the publisher.

First edition 2021

Library of Congress Catalog Card Number pending
ISBN 978-1-5362-0891-7

20 21 22 23 24 25 LEO 10 9 8 7 6 5 4 3 2 1

Printed in Heshan, Guangdong, China

This book was typeset in Mrs. Eaves.
The illustrations were done in colored pencil and gouache.

Candlewick Press
99 Dover Street
Somerville, Massachusetts 02144

www.candlewick.com